How I Met My Dog

How I Met My Dog

BRICK D HINKLEY

iUniverse LLC
Bloomington

How I Met My Dog

iUniverse books may be ordered through booksellers or by contacting:

iUniverse LLC
1663 Liberty Drive
Bloomington, IN 47403
www.iuniverse.com
1-800-Authors (1-800-288-4677)

ISBN: 978-1-4759-6985-6 (sc)
ISBN: 978-1-4759-6986-3 (ebk)

Printed in the United States of America

iUniverse rev. date: 08/29/2013

Once upon a time there lived to two kids that lived with their dad .
One day they they decided to go for a walk they asked their dad if it was okay .

Dad said " Sure but be careful."
girl said " We will Dad ."
boy said " Lets go sis ."
She replied eagerly " Okay ."

The two of them walked for a few minutes .

After walking for a few minutes ,

They saw a bench and decided to stop for a rest .

" This a nice place for a rest " Comment The brother ."

They sat down to take a rest .

" I hear something in the bushes " replied the sister .Both children looked over to the bushes

He questioned her " What do you think it is ?"

sis Answered, " What ever it is it is coming from those bushes .'

" I think it sounds like a dog " the boy stated

They both went over to bush to check the sound and discover a dog that was tangled up in branches .

It took them a while but they were able to untangle it "

Sister said " Let's take the dog home .

I think he must be thirsty and hungry"

brother agreed " Okay ."

She then commented " I wonder where his owner is ?"

They looked around the park and saw that no one was there .

While the kids were walking home they were discussing what to do with the dog .

Sister said "I hope that Dad lets us keep the dog ."

Brother replied " Don't get mad if dad doesn't let you keep it ."

The two children arived home and found out that there was no one at home .

She said " Dad we are home, come and see what we found in the park ."

Brother said " You get some water while I tie up the dog out side ok."

" Okay I will ."

She then got the water for the dog .

It was getting close to supper time . Dad decided to go and find the kids .

Dad said " It is getting close to supper time I better go and find them ."

He then headed in the direction the kids had gone in .

Knowing that the children often go to the park . Dad went to the park to get them ,But they had already went home .

" They are not here . I Better check if they have gone home." He then headed back home.

When dad arrived home he saw the dog in the yard
He said " I wonder which friend
they found in the park today ?" He then went into the house .

Dad walked in the door and saw his two children sitting at the table .

Dad said " Who's dog is that tied up in the yard ?"

the children then looked at each other before the

Son said " We are not sure . We found him in the park and brought him home ."

Daughter said " Daddy can we keep him ?"

Father thought for a few moments before answering his daughter .

He said " I know that you always wanted a dog . But it might belong to some one else ok dear ."

Daughter said " I guess so dad ." as she looked down sadly .

The two children then went out on to the streets in order to find put who owned the dog .

Not liking this she commented by saying hopefully " I hope that we do not find it's owner ."

Brother replied " Some kid might be missing thier dog ."

" I know . I know big brother . I still wish that i can keep the dog ."

They then continued to put up posters .

Found

Some time later a man comes to the house.

the stranger said " Are you the ones that put up this poster . "

Father said " Yes it is , is that your dog that we had found . "

" Found it found it you stole it ."

"We did not steal your dog . "

" Yes you did and I want you to give it back ."

After watch his dad talking to the
stranger . He did not have a good
feeling about what he saw.
brother said " There is some one
talking to dad out there ."
Sister said " Who is it ?"
" i am not sure but I don't
like the looks of him ."
" Do you think he is the dog's owner ?"
" I hope he is not but I am afraid that
he is ."

Being afraid of the man that had come to the house she went out the back door.Talkinq to the doq .

Sister said " I hope that you are not his dog . Are you his dog ? Don't tell me if you are ok ."

She then just sat their and stroked the dogs back .

The two are discussing about the dog . When he comes to tell his father that his sister had gone away with the dog .

the man said " Well go and find your sister . Before I call the cops you little punk ."

father said " Mister just wait moment while I talk to my son." The father turned to his son ." Do you know where your sister has gone to ? "

the boy looked at him for a moment before answering .

He said " No . But i will go and look for her ."

man said " You should go and hurry up and find the brat ."

A few minutes later the two children return with the dog

man said " You two took my dog I want you to give it back "

Sister said " We did not steal it . We found it in the park."

man said " NO no you took my dog . "

boy said " why are you calling me and my sister thiefs ?"

man said " I had the dog tied up in my back yard ."

girl said " mister we found the dog in the park . "

The man then looked at the 2 kids for a few moments he then smiled for a moment .

boy said nerversley " What do you want mister.

You are scaring me and my sister ."

man said " Do you like my dog kid ."

she reply " I think it is a nice dog ."

"want to buy him ." the kids were stunned and didn't respond.

The man and the kids then discussed the purchase of the dog .After a while they agreed that she would have to earn the money to buy the dog . After the man left the 2 kids continued talking .

Brother said " Sis do you think can do it ?"

Sister said " I hope so brother remember that you can not help me ."

"He won't know if i do ."

" Okay i wil not help you ."

" Here i go with my
first job ."

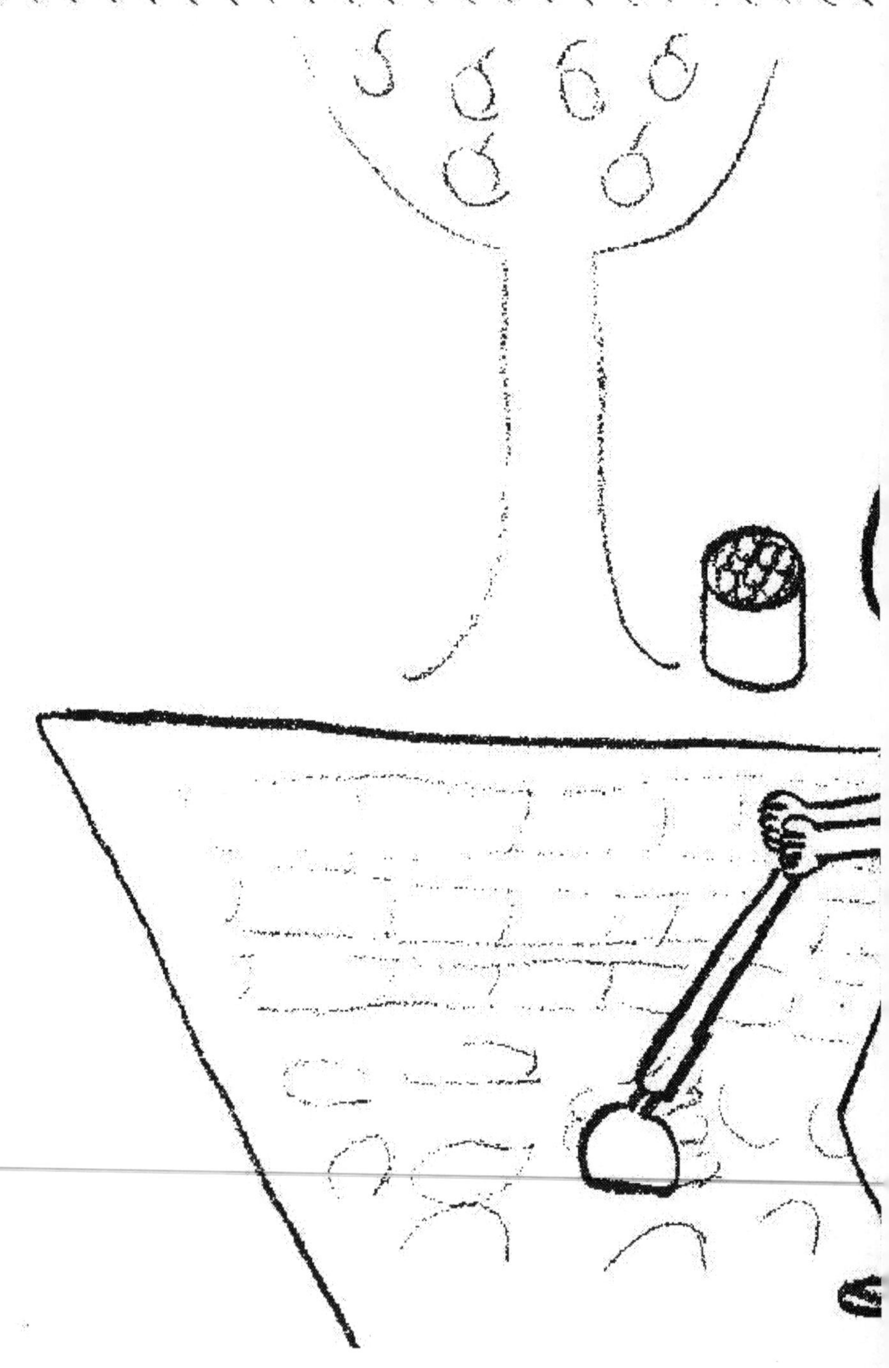

Brother said "How is it going ."
Sister said " Great making lots of money ."
" Good , I found a fence that needs painting if you want to earns the money."
" You know you are not suppose to me helping me ."
" I am not you will still be doing all of the work sis ."

She Said to her self " Painting fences can certainly a messy thing to do. When i finished a nice long bath seem like a good idea ."

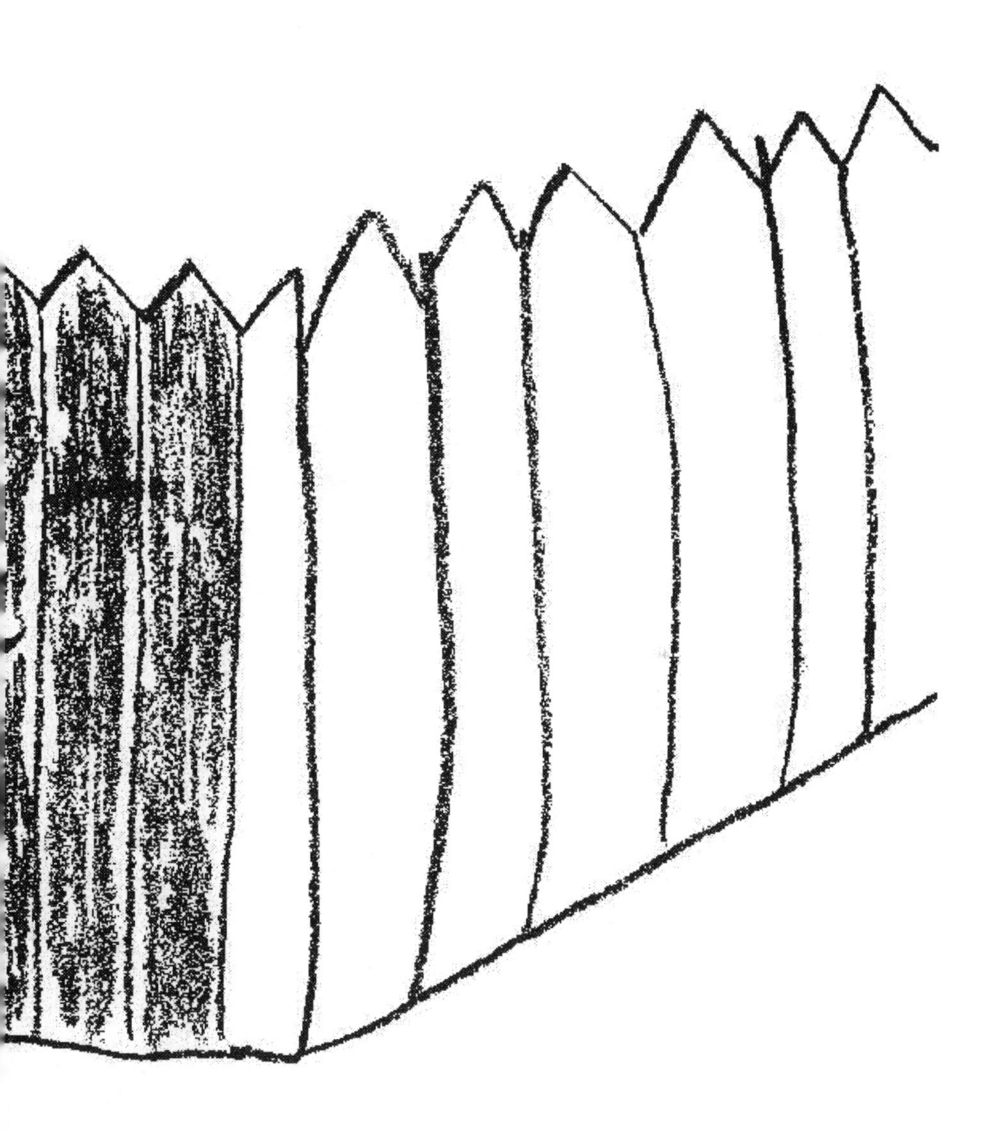

After the children had just finished their baths. They were in the kitchen counting how much money she had earned in the past week . When their dad walks into the room.

Dad said " Have you earned enough money for the dog yet ?"

sister said " i am getting very close dad . I think I will have enough money by the weekend ."

After a week or so of earning money to buy the dog . She had reached her goal and just finishing up her last task .

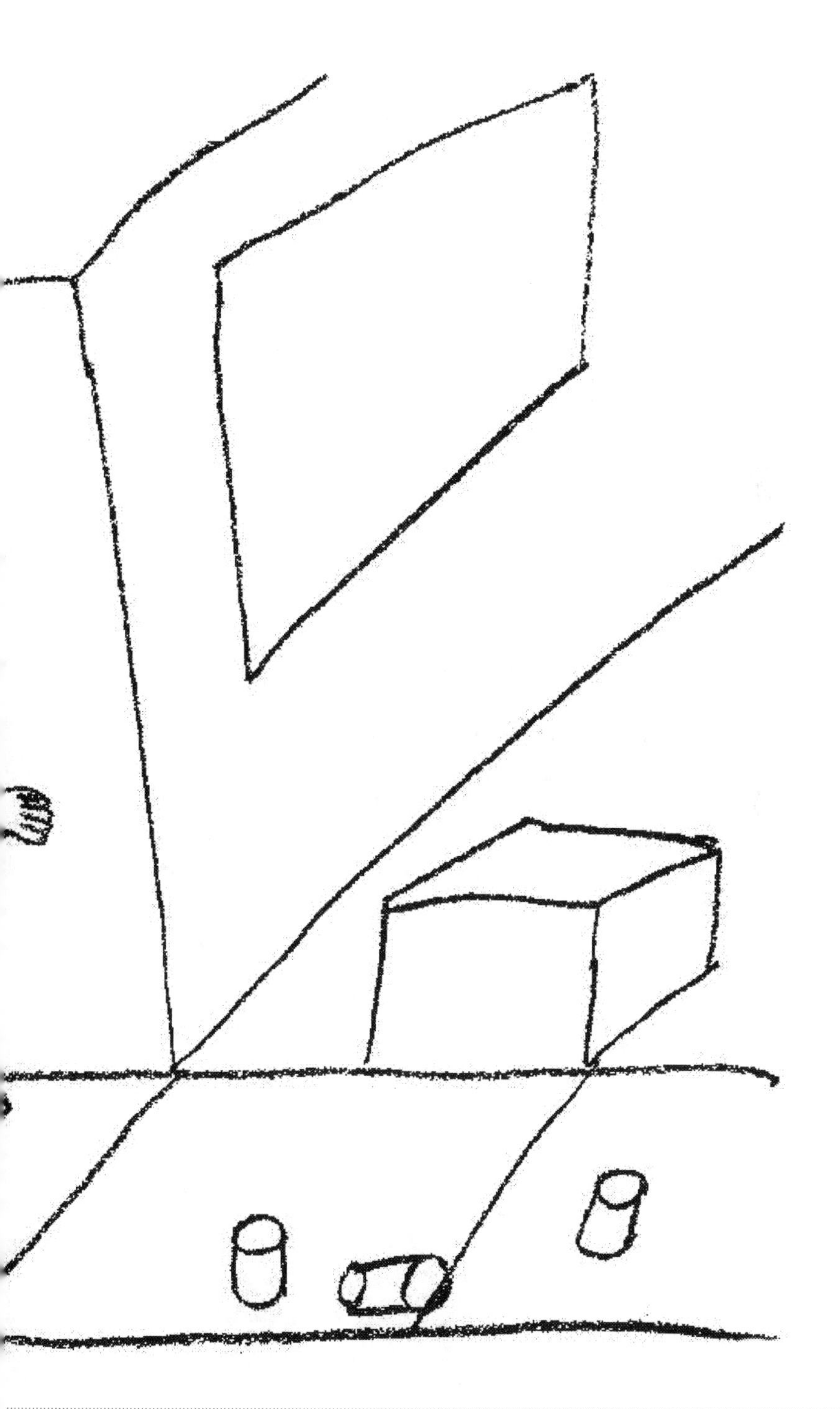

She had finally earned enough money to buy the dog. But when she was about to recieved a nasty surpise .

she said " Here I have the money for the dog ."

dog owner said " I am sorry but the dog ran away . If you want the dog you will have to find it ourself."

" Here is the money for the dog mister ."

He looked at her and said " No you keep the money you'll need it for dog food and stuff ."

"Why did you want me earn the money if you didn't want it ."

" I wanted to see how much you wanted the dog ."

" Thanks for the dog mister ."

She went back to where she and her brother had found the dog . Unfortunate the dog was not there . She was not sure where to look for the dog next and thought about where to look next.

After she had looked all over town trying to find the dog . She went to the dog pound to ask if any one had turned the dog in .

She said " I am looking for my dog has any one turned him in yet ?"

lady said " Does he have a dog tag ?"

" No he doesn't I just bought him today from his owner ."

" Sorry no one has turned in a dog today ."

" Thanks ."

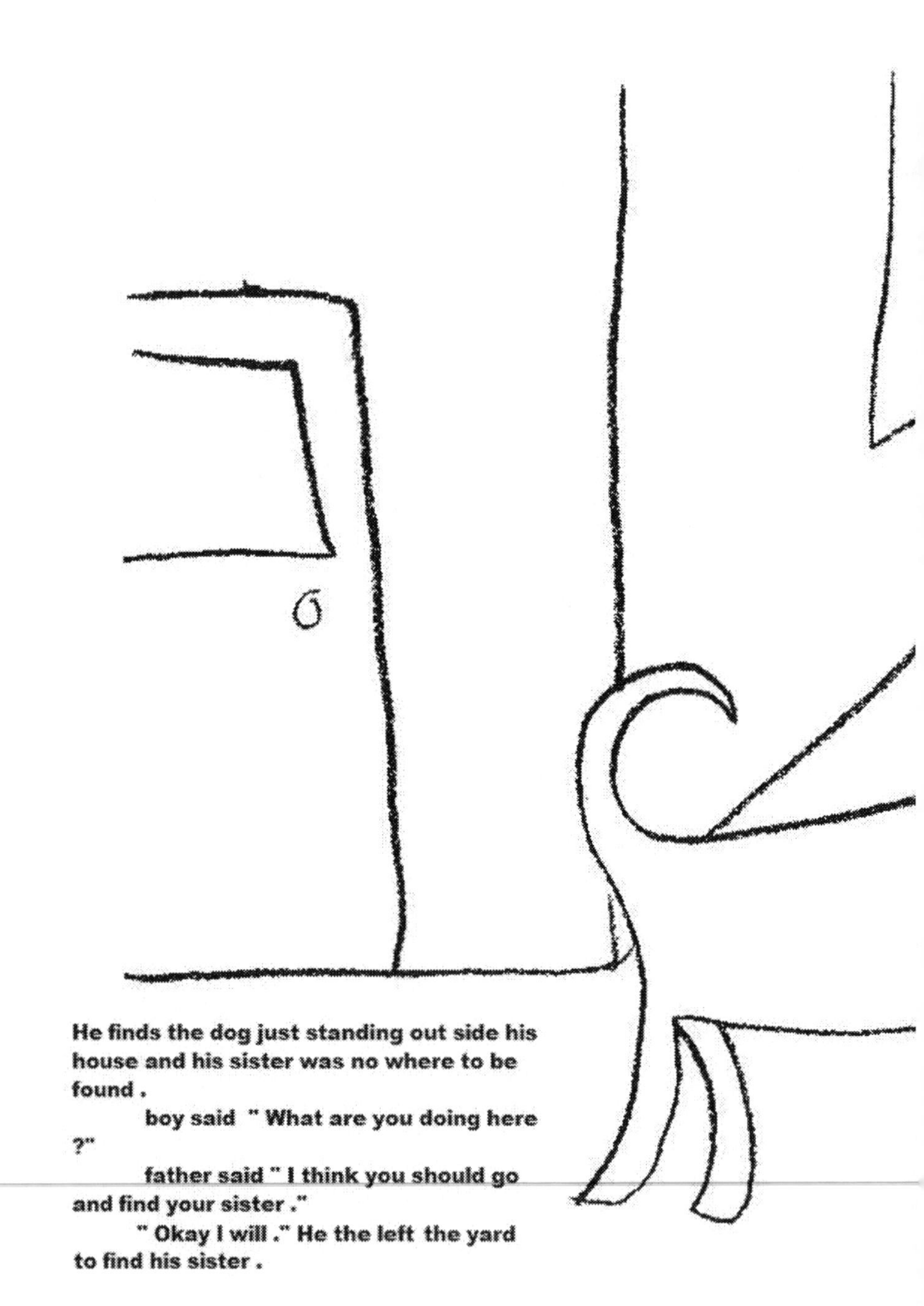

He finds the dog just standing out side his house and his sister was no where to be found .

boy said " What are you doing here ?"

father said " I think you should go and find your sister ."

" Okay I will ." He the left the yard to find his sister .

Brother said " look who just showed up at the house ."
Sister said " brother i am so happy ."
" did you pay the man for the dog ."
" he didn't want the money ."
" why not ?"
" He told me that i could use the money to take care of the dog ."

Printed in the United States
By Bookmasters